# DR. HERZOG'S COLLECTION

ROBERT BAGNALL

Published by Graveside Press
graveside-press.com



Editing: Poppy McDonald, Kelley York
Cover illustration: Sleepy Fox Studio
Interior Formatting: Sleepy Fox Studio

Digital 978-1-969655-22-7
Paperback (Trade) 978-1-969655-21-0

**No part of this book has been created using Generative AI. Graveside Press and its authors do not consent for our works to be utilized in any form of machine learning training.**

GRAVESIDE PRESS

# CONTENT NOTES

*For a list of potentially triggering content,*
*please skip to page 48.*

TINY TERRORS
short
stories

In my dreams, I see Doctor Herzog pivot over the railing of his balcony. Flailing like a rag doll into the darkness, limbs akimbo.

He hits the spiked iron railing dividing his property from the street below, skewered at the spine.

Suddenly he is stock still, like a statue. Just his eyeballs rolling. Snowflakes settling on his face, white against white hair.

And then his collection, his precious collection, fluttering down seconds later, one plastering itself over his face, as though dead eyes could still read. Gazing down, I can almost make out the words. Some nights I think I can, if only I could get a fraction closer. I can almost discern the spider-like signature on the letter. I can see each and every hair and eyelash. So why can't I read what is written?

In this dream, euphoria washes over me. Elation at what I've done.

But I know, objectively, logically, I'm too far away, too high up to pick out those details. And, anyway, it's far too dark. So, I know these are just fantasies, the products of delirium played out in my mind.

Other nights, I'm trying to stop him from jumping. Pleading with him. But I can't hear my own voice. I don't know what I'm saying, but I know I'm trying to help him. But it's too late. He throws open the window and, with the deft, flowing movements of a dancer, jumps.

I'm at the window, craning out, looking down with a sick revulsion as he falls in slow motion. The result is the same, but I don't stare. I turn away in a blind fury, my bile rising.

Sometimes there are people with me. I am not alone. But their faces never come into focus. They are always just beyond my sight. I suspect they are people I have met since. So, these dreams must represent the least likely scenario.

But how do I know? I'm sick. These days, everybody's sick.

***

I had taken lodgings near the docks. My rooms smelled of tallow and fish stew and sweat soaked leather. Steam hammers struck over and over in the middle distance. I shared a tiny garret, all steel and glass and smooth artificial surfaces in the late Pre-Pulse style when we could still build like that, with my trunk and its few contents.

Occasionally, I would play cards in the back room of an inn. Win a little, lose a little, but never give away my name or history. I felt estranged from the place of my birth, of my boyhood adventures, where my condition first manifested itself. Perhaps I simply did not want to be reminded. Perhaps I had come back to die. Perhaps my reasons were not that complicated.

I had no visitors and few people to visit. Other than those who had to for reasons of business, nobody knew I was in the city. Few were even aware I was in the country. Or so I believed, until two events in close succession showed that I was wrong.

The first was a letter, hand delivered to my lodgings with my full name, Jonathan Cartier, written in a flowing hand on the envelope. It had arrived whilst I sauntered aimlessly through the wharves, a shadow quickly forgotten by the stevedores. I could get nothing out of the old woman who was employed to cook and clean. She had seen nothing. Did I think she had time to watch for comings and goings? She would get nothing done that way. The Devil makes work for idle hands.

I broke the wax seal—a touch I found equally theatrical, pretentious, and preposterous—with foreboding. Inside was a single buff-colored card, on which was written in a neat gothic hand, *Doctor Cornelius Herzog requests the pleasure of your company on...*

The second event took the form of a trench-coated figure in the doorway. The card still in my hand, I silently cursed being too absorbed to have ensured the door was fully closed. The man leant on the doorframe, conscious he did not, strictly speaking, have the right to enter my room.

"Somebody has a sense of history," he said, motioning towards the broken red wax. "It's been a long time since I saw anybody seal a letter like that. Maybe only in children's stories."

"Have you come to arrest me, Inspector?" I said as evenly as I could. "I understood the matter to be closed."

"I don't think you would have returned if you thought that was a possibility. It was taken out of my hands long ago. My job is not without politics. It is like swimming in a sea of shit. You can only ever see so much. But there are questions I would like to ask, for my own satisfaction."

As I had not asked Inspector Bertrand to leave, he assumed he was free to enter. He propped himself against the breakfast bar of the open plan studio, glancing down at the city through the dirty plate-glass windows.

"For example, and I'm taking it as read that you killed him," he waved away any objections on my part, "how did you know that Kristian was about to embezzle you? I've been over it in forensic detail. I cannot work it out. You cannot possibly have known at the point he was killed."

"I didn't know."

"But you killed him. Then you ran away. Why? What other motive could you have had? You must have known. But, simultaneously, you couldn't have done."

My forehead throbbed, a single isolated point just above my right eye, slightly towards my temple. "I didn't know."

Bertrand smiled. We both knew I hadn't denied killing Kristian.

"I think there are good things that came out of the Pulse, you know." He nodded at the letter.

"Writing letters?" I could not hide my incredulity. "Hundreds of millions died. Maybe billions."

"Not letters as such. But somebody has to make the paper. Somebody has to make the ink. Somebody has to make the shoe leather of the person who delivers it. What I can't work out is what everybody used to do before the Pulse. People do things with their hands now. It's better."

He had a point. "I traveled with a man called DeSouza. He had a theory about why everybody is so damned miserable. It's because all the books survived. Books are old technology, but they describe a golden age. We can still read about sending messages in an instant to somebody half a world away or holding machines in your hand that can tell you where you are, anywhere in the world, down to the nearest finger width. But we have returned to a world of ink pens and sealing wax. That's why he thought everybody is the way they are."

"I have a handheld in a box somewhere," Bertrand mused. "Useless thing. My grandfather's, I think. Maybe my wife's grandfather's."

"There are people who collect them."

"There are always people who collect useless things."

"Or things that can't be made use of."

He smiled, almost laughed at my allusion to the information he sought, and with that he was gone.

I looked back at the card. Doctor Herzog. It was two years since I had seen him. In fact, the last day I saw him was also the last time I saw Inspector Bertrand. It was a short meeting, in Bertrand's office rather than the interrogation room. There was a view of the church from it. The atmosphere had altered. No more the mental chess match, Bertrand trying to extract a confession by means of leaving me no logical alternative other than to admit my guilt. He didn't know whether to sit or stand, a foot on his chair, fingers tapping a letter on the leather-topped desk.

"Vassily has withdrawn his statement," he said.

"What does that mean?"

"Why would Vassily do that?"

"What does that mean for me?" I asked.

"It means that you're free to go. But why would Vassily do that?"

I did not furnish him with a response. Instead, I went straight to Doctor Herzog's office. His nurse opened the door. She knew me well by sight. Moments later, Herzog came out of his consulting room, wiping his hands on a towel. I had no idea why he did that. All he had to do for his patients was listen to them.

"I'm leaving the city," I said.

Herzog raised an enquiring eyebrow.

"So, obviously, I am discharging myself as your patient."

"Do you think that's wise? Your condition has shown little sign of improvement."

"Exactly why a change is a good idea. A warmer climate. They've opened South America again. I thought I'd go there."

Herzog paused, adopting the friendly, calming doctor's voice as though trying on a more appropriate tie. "Jon, we're talking about episodes of violence associated with prolonged mental blackouts. Not a bad head cold."

"I came to inform you of a decision. Not to seek advice."

"Even so, as your doctor..."

"You are no longer my doctor," I snapped.

After that, I do not remember what happened. The next I knew, I was walking along a wide avenue, an autumn breeze catching the leaves. My head throbbed with the hangover of recent anger, but my knuckles were not chaffed, my forearms were not strained from punching. I concluded I had simply left.

However, I had departed Doctor Herzog's office, I had clearly not killed him, and never once thought that was likely, as here he was, two years later, inviting me to dinner. Herzog and Bertrand, book-ending the last two years of my life.

I find it hard to describe how I felt looking at Herzog's invitation. Irritation bordering on anger that he had found me. And, if both he and Bertrand were aware I was here, who else knew? I was inclined to throw the note into the black waters of the docks, to pretend I had never even received it. But then a subtler plan occurred to me. The doctor was well off. Even in the emotional turmoil of our sessions, I remembered picking out those telltale details: the cut of his suit, the mirror polish of his shoes, the easy manner that only comes from a comfortable situation. I no longer represented a good risk to any bank or official moneylender here. The doctor, however, may have been given to thinking in terms more honorable, more gentlemanly, than collateral and cumulative interest.

Maybe I could touch him for money.

That night by the light of a candle I wrote a short letter accepting his invitation, adding that it would be good to see him after so long and that, hopefully, I would find him in good spirits. Then I studied his original note and wondered how I could read so little into it. Just a yearning, an uneasiness. And a hope for the future based on little but faith. But nothing more.

***

The curious aspect of my decision to withdraw from Doctor Herzog's treatment was that it initially proved correct. The blackouts, the evidence of violence, my violence, which I kept finding afterwards—all of it vanished.

But it had been replaced by something far stranger.

My strongest recollections of the day I left were the heavy thumps of wet ropes against the hull as we slipped our moorings. The sudden sway underfoot as the tethered beast was given its freedom. The calls from the harbor hands, the shouted instructions. A family waving for the benefit of one of the other passengers, the father in a dark suit, his raised arm static, palm open, as though trying to catch the chair's eye at a public meeting. The mother, face intent, mouth agog, holding down a hat in the spring breeze with one hand, gesticulating in fits and starts with the other, as if attracting a waiter.

I watched them until the ship reached the mouth of the harbor and the swell of the open sea kicked in. They turned and went, as did I. I had no family to see me off. They believed I had killed Kristian and, whilst willing to pay off Vassily, were unwilling to let me back into their bosom. I was banished, exiled.

When I emerged onto deck again, having been unable to read in a swell that would no doubt only get worse, we had left the coast far behind. All that remained of my home was a gray-black tongue between the blue-gray of the sky and the gray-blue of the sea. Never before had I left land, not in any significant sense. Now, I would not see it again for almost a month.

There were five other passengers. Ravette was a burly, bearded engineer who had spent four years repairing the highway network in the Balkans, expanding both cobble top and charging points. He was now under contract to do the same for another three in Mexico. Oil and gas had long since run out. Wells and refineries that escaped the firestorms following the sudden, savage solar activity were destroyed in the ensuing civil unrest. That, or they eventually ran dry. The Pulse made all prospecting equipment more sophisticated than a literal stab in the dark inoperative. There were minor shallow strikes, but anything dependent on oil or gas, even if it could live without a silicon chip to control it, quickly went thirsty. The roads became deserted, many returning to nature or becoming narrow strips for horse carts and thieves.

Over the decades, people became used to living with the Pulse, a misnomer, as it made it sound like a singular event rather than a continual bombarding stream of solar energy. Machines could run on electricity—there was plenty of that to be had, generated from wind and wave and, the root cause of all our problems, the sun, or even steam—but now they were guided by human minds and hands. "Digital" reverted to its previously archaic status as a term relating to the fingers. Sixty years after the Pulse began, industry had pulled itself up sufficiently to produce crude electric cars and trains in numbers. The city-states of Europe began to reform into nation-states, which meant the joining up of long abandoned highways and railroads. That was Ravette's world.

A brooding man, given to treating even the most minor decision with the furrowed brows of a weighty dilemma, he was the first of my fellow travelers that I tried to engage in any real conversation. I discovered he was not a man for geeing up spirits. He would sit hunched, holding his tin mug of coffee with his fingertips, talking in a monotone as his eyes bored into the table.

Collier was the opposite of Ravette, a surgeon who had accepted an appointment at a Guadalajara hospital without the slightest knowledge of what lay in store for him. He reasoned anything into which he threw himself impulsively could be as easily escaped. Admirable, if misguided.

He and I shared bottles of rough spirit distilled by the crew from the heat of the engine and innumerable card games. He was not a player. Games would end in polite confusion with cards accidentally overturned in the deal, coins thrown off the table by the swell, misunderstandings over calls and rules. He would throw up his hands in mock horror and insist on finances being returned to how they had been at the outset. By such means, the clock could always be turned back on divisive chaos.

The third and fourth passengers were nuns, Sisters Marie and Angelica. They avoided contact with all of us, save nodded smiles at mealtimes. They ate together, not just in the trivial sense of at the same time in the same place, but in unison. Their spoons would raise soup to their lips at the same time. They would dab the corners of their mouths as one. They would finish neck and neck. And when they finished, they would get up, smile at us, and leave. I never heard them speak. They had been sent to the Americas. As people voluntarily seeking to travel to a continent only recently, and somewhat dubiously, declared clean, I think they regarded us as unconvertible heathens. As such, we stood diametrically opposite to those born in the Americas and thus susceptible to the Good Book.

DeSouza made up our number. It had been his family waving farewell from the quayside. He was "off to seek his fortune". The kind of phrase which would have Collier laughing and pouring more brandy but drive Ravette to deeper brooding. At twenty-two, DeSouza was six years younger than me. He had wiry black hair and a moon face with features crowded into the middle, as if for safety, beneath wire-rimmed glasses.

It was DeSouza who, unwittingly, demonstrated the strange direction in which my condition had progressed. I had slept deeply, even though the ship had pitched and yawed in the night. I had grown quite accustomed to its movements, and a night playing brag with Collier and

DeSouza had helped. Indeed, I had slept so deeply I had missed breakfast. Sunlight was flooding my cabin when I awoke, my head thick with the previous night's brandy and tobacco.

Having failed to rouse me, DeSouza had pushed a note under my cabin door. Somewhere in a dream, I remembered staccato hammering. The note itself was quite simple—*Gone for a walk, De.S*. But as soon as I read it, nausea washed over me. I felt a blinding pain behind my eyes. Giddy, I sunk to my haunches to stop myself falling, and saw DeSouza making his way through the engine room, along a metal walkway between the two engines, waving and sharing a joke with the engineers, just as a steam pipe exploded sending out a rivet with the velocity of a rifle bullet straight at him.

It was not a fleeting vision. In it, DeSouza took his time descending the ladder to the engine room, looked about, took a firm grasp of the handrails and pulled himself against the pitch of the boat towards his doom. As steam enveloped DeSouza's toppling body, the image vanished. It had not been in any way unclear. Nor was it an interpretation; there were no signs to be "read into" in this hallucination. It was all right before my eyes, as sharp as if I were there, watching the scene myself. I knew as a plain and simple fact that it was not a vision of the past or the present, but of the immediate future.

I threw myself at my cabin door, still dressed in a nightshirt, tumbling along the passageway towards the thick iron hatch that led outside. Cold mid-ocean air rushed into my lungs. A rating gasped at my comic appearance. I almost lost my footing on the wet deck. Keeping one hand within catching distance of the grab rail, I ran for the engine room where DeSouza was about to descend. Although officially off limits, we had become friendly with the engineers. DeSouza had a habit of paying the engine room a visit most mornings. He must have been deep in thought, as he only saw me when I made a lunge for him.

We both spoke at once:

"Cartier?"

"DON'T."

I clung to him by the shoulder. I can't imagine what I looked like, barefoot in mid-Atlantic, raving.

"Don't go down there."

"What the hell do you mean?"

"Don't go down there. There's going to be an accident. One of the boilers is going to explode. A rivet...a rivet..."

DeSouza exploded with laughter. "Cartier. Look at yourself. I go down here every morning. A couple of times around deck, down below, and then back out to smell the salt again."

He pulled himself away from my grasp, taking in the full horror of my appearance, shaking his head with a sardonic smile. "It clears the head of the brandy. You should try it."

As he took a couple of steps down the ladder, what sounded like the crack of a rifle came from the engine room, followed by the scream of escaping steam. Voices raised in panic followed, instructions barked in a Slavic tongue I did not recognize. DeSouza froze on the ladder, head and shoulders above deck, as steam billowed up around him. In an instant, one of the engineers had ushered him out and the hatch had been slammed behind him.

He looked ashen. "If I hadn't paused... You knew. How did you know?"

I did not reply. I couldn't. Even if I could find the words, the cold, the shock, the rolling of the boat all added up and I was violently sick over the side.

***

DeSouza treated my premonition with a detached empiricism I found alarming. That evening, he set up an experiment with the pack of cards. He shuffled several times, held up each card in succession, the face away from me, and asked me to name the suit. I decided to entertain him and gave the first answer that came into my head, not even thinking to ensure thirteen of each. Halfway through, I remembered clubs, so I gave him five or six in a row to compensate.

"Fourteen. Near enough random. If this were under true experimental conditions, I would, of course, repeat it to ensure veracity. However, I fear that would tax your patience."

I drummed my fingers on the tabletop and listened to the ocean as he wrote a line of Shakespeare on a piece of paper and asked me to read it. No visions came to me. No blinding pain. No nausea. They were just words on paper.

He then repeated the experiment. Again, I gave an answer, no more than an arbitrary guess, to each card. At the end, he put the pack down and stared at the ground blankly.

"Well?"

He looked me in the eye, over the top of his glasses. His expression was quizzical. "Thirty-three."

"Luck."

He shook his head. "Twenty, maybe. Twenty-six, half the pack. That would be luck in its most extreme form. But not thirty-three. You have a gift. I believe you can tell a person's immediate future from their handwriting. Subliminally, much of the time, but when the future is shocking, it rises into consciousness."

"That's ridiculous."

"Thirty-three," he reminded me.

***

Doctor Herzog's flat fronted townhouse had been built in a brutal architectural style. The lower ground floor, sunk partly below the level of the pavement, gave the house the air of having something to hide. A narrow trench, which allowed the windows of the lowest floor a sliver of natural light, was bounded from the road by a wrought-iron fence with spiked finials. Three granite steps led up to the main door on the floor above. It was a common design in this part of the city.

It was dark when I arrived, swirling drizzle hanging in the air, too thick for mist, too light to be rain. The temperature was dropping rapidly. It would turn to snow before long. I had been there many times before, but in the middle of the day, as the doctor preferred to start his sessions mid-morning and finish mid-afternoon, allowing him to complete the day's paperwork at his leisure. Standing on the step listening to the hollow echo of the door chime reminded me of the sunny days I came as a patient, but only as a stylized portrait reminds one of the sitter. There was a resemblance rather than an exact likeness. I was not coming back to the place of my attempted cure. That place was one of bright golden stone, warm summer air, and the scent of flowers. This place was gray and damp, dimly lit. I was merely coming back to a reminder of that place. It somehow made it easier to separate past and present, easier to bear.

Whereas once Herzog's nurse would have opened the door, it was now his wife who greeted me. She smiled as though she knew me well, although I honestly could not recall ever meeting her. However, during my treatment, Herzog frequently mentioned her. She had trained in psychiatry as well. Herzog had been her tutor. I wondered if they had discussed my file.

My hat and coat, for which I had been so grateful while walking the winter streets, were gathered away. Herzog, the cliché of a Viennese psychiatrist, bushy white whiskers and wiry pebble glasses, bounded toward me, hand outstretched.

"How are you, my dear Cartier?" He beamed, pumping my hand, beckoning me towards an easy chair into which I gently lowered myself. Herzog remained standing, leaning against the mantelpiece, perhaps to maintain a superior position, looking down from above.

"Are you asking as a doctor?"

He guffawed. "As a friend. Your treatment finished two years ago, at least. There have been no…" He waved a hand expressively before him. "No repeat occurrences?"

I shook my head. There was no need to give away anything I didn't have to.

"I was surprised to learn you were in the city."

"They opened South America up too early. The revolutions. I had to return."

"I meant more that you had returned here rather than left there. Why, I am forgetting myself," he said, his humor far too forced. "I have yet to offer you a drink."

He sauntered across the room towards a table weighed down with cut glass. Dinner parties, I reminded myself, habitually begin with forced jollity before alcohol works as a lubricant and catalyst. There was nothing unusual in the doctor's manner. I was being foolish.

There were four of us for dinner. "Darton's father owns a shipping line," Herzog said obliquely, by way of introduction.

"Shipping lines. And a bank. And a solar plant."

Darton had arrived late, jabbering apologies. Herzog watched him with fatherly concern and indulgence. His wife, on the other hand, wore an enigmatic expression. I suspected she had met him before and it had not been altogether pleasant. He had the air of a man who chose his words carefully but was still taken by surprise at what came out.

If I had to sum up Darton in one word, it would be *fraud*. Most people who are crudely labeled mad—the depressed, the befuddled, the simple—do not exhibit the symptoms of madness as you would find them played out for laughs. Madness, in my experience, takes the form of eyes staring inwards, inertia to the point of coma. Or panic. Or rocking, rocking back and forth. Flicking, flickering eyes searching for an answer somewhere nearby but only finding demons. Or violence, short, swift, and brutal. Madness does not take the form of Darton's eyes seeking reaction, of giggles, of a finger run around the inside of the mouth followed by somber gnomic declarations. That is nothing more than a parody of madness, a caricature of affliction. But they were the symptoms that Darton displayed. And if *I* knew he was faking, then surely so did the doctor.

The meal was sumptuous, skillfully prepared by Herzog's wife. I saw no signs of any servants in the house. Herzog said something about his wife enjoying the preparation of food and having sent the staff home to have the run of the kitchen. I found this a strange arrangement in such a house on such a night but could see no reason to question it.

Helping himself to more vegetables, Herzog explained for Darton's benefit that I was the owner of an important South American business.

"Hardly," I replied.

"Silver mine, was it not?"

"Ice. We made ice. But I am not really sure whether I am still the part-owner."

"Come, come. You either are, or you are not. Which is it?"

"Well," I wrung my hands. I had not expected an interrogation. "Technically, I am. But the revolution..."

"Revolutions go around," Darton interjected, exploding with mirth at his joke. "What goes around comes around back again. But, be warned, it soon goes away again."

"I mean the revolution came and I had to leave."

I tried to make it sound matter of fact enough to satisfy Herzog's curiosity. But it wasn't. He removed his glasses and began to clean them, using the ruse to casually probe further.

"Where was it, remind me? Brazil?"

"No. Not Brazil."

"Mexico?"

"We landed in Mexico. But we caught a second ship, another cargo vessel, *The Cardinal*, which took us further south, to South America proper. And then by rail and mule further inland."

I tried to make it sound throwaway, to stifle questions, but this was just the prelude to the merry dance I would no doubt have to go through many times more as people woke up to my return. "You'll forgive me if I do not feel eager to talk about it."

"So, you've returned rich. Is that it?" Herzog was suddenly hearty and hale-fellow-well-met. "You've returned a rich man, and you don't want to boast." He slapped the table. "We quite understand."

His remark was aimed at prying open my recent history, hopefully leading to an adventurous tale modestly told. But there was no such ripping yarn. Only shame.

"Cornelius." His wife laid a gentle hand over her husband's.

"I've heard there are hills made out of gold," Darton shot. "Hills out of gold. So big, so solid, that you can't mine them because they're so big, so solid." Darton spoke like he did not have enough breath for a whole sentence.

I smiled wanly and shook my head. "We made ice. Ice." I repeated the key word, as though it may help get the message through to Darton.

"I hear you're bankrupt," Darton suddenly shot at Herzog.

The three of us had our knives and forks poised in mid-air, food hanging before our mouths. We froze, all staring at Darton, who had a look of smug satisfaction on his face, of a checkmate achieved, the truth of which has yet to register with his opponent.

Doctor Herzog's wife, in contrast, wore the expression I had seen before at the kangaroo courts dotted about revolutionary South America. It was the look that came to a woman when their son or husband was condemned to hang. But, whilst those glassy stares would break into uncontrolled and uncontrollable hysterics, here it hung motionless on her face, just as the corpses hung by the time dusk fell.

"Let us not talk of such things," Herzog said after a moment.

"No. I disagree. Let's talk," Darton said pleasantly. Malicious words delivered devoid of malice. "You, Mr. Cartier. Are you a bankrupt?"

"I have no idea."

Herzog's wife let out an involuntary laugh at my words, although they were not meant to be humorous.

"What do you mean, you have no idea?"

It was like dealing with a child. "I mean, the revolution came, and I had to leave my assets behind."

"The ice?" He leered towards me. "That will have melted by now."

***

DeSouza looked after the technical aspects of the business, the quality of the salts the Indians brought by mule from San Juan, the building of the ice-making machines, and so forth. I was the negotiator, the persuader, the oiler of palms. DeSouza found himself liable to give ground at the slightest opportunity, not through being weak willed, just too eager to please.

Of course, I had one important advantage over him in negotiations. I only had to ask for clarification of an offer or condition in writing to judge whether to press further or concede my position. My gift had remained with me following the voyage, although never again in the crystal-clear form it had taken when DeSouza had escaped the accident in the engine room. I had come to think of his hypothesis of how my "gift" worked as accurate. I rarely saw the immediate future of the author. Instead, the shape of things to come was told to me through a sweet taste on my tongue, or through the sweat on my palms. Sometimes an iron hand would grip my stomach. On other occasions, I would feel myself rising with elation, as though I were being lifted off the ground. Objects before my eyes would recede or rush towards me. Colors would sharpen. Voices were lost in a universal, all-encompassing hum, like massive machinery heard far away.

Occasionally, my premonitions would come close to my experience onboard ship. Once, DeSouza had agreed to write to the wholesaler in San Juan complaining about the short measures of salt arriving on mule-back. He passed his draft note, somewhat terse and direct, by me. He had a habit of wanting to prove he could be assertive, whilst seeking my diplomatic softening of his tone. As soon as I saw his spidery scrawl, it was as if I had been struck on the back of the head. I felt sick. I had the taste of hot sour bile on the back of my throat.

"The ice," I gasped. "The ice is poisoned."

"Poisoned?" said DeSouza. "But you haven't eaten any ice?"

"It was the note," I said, dazed. "I got it from the note. The ice will be poisoned tomorrow. You would have been poisoned."

The next day we caught the man as he dropped something into the container which held the water whilst it froze. It was a coarse gray powder and, almost certainly, would not have been visible through the gray semi-translucent ice.

The foreman, a son of the Indian chief, looked at the powder, tasted it on a dampened fingertip, and declared it to be "juca" beaten to a rough powder. When we said we had never heard of it, he looked darkly at us as though we were imbeciles. We discovered that juca was nothing more than a type of sweet potato that, uncooked, would induce stomach cramps but could potentially kill. He insisted the authorities should not be informed and that the tribe be left to deal with their own. We never discovered what happened to the poisoner. If anything.

It was a month later, on the third consecutive day the Indians failed to turn up to work the machines, that I finally knew it was all too late. The Indians had gone from San Marco, not just from the factory. Melted into the forest like ice left in the sunshine.

DeSouza handed me another draft communication, this time to our embassy in the capital. I do not remember whether it was a plea for protection or a strident broadside against the actions or inactions of the government. All I recall is the strangest feeling the document generated in me. It was as though I was conscious of void, of emptiness, of utter vacuum, of dreamless sleep. I can only put it in weak metaphors and poor similes. I had seen nothingness in utter clarity, but knew it meant DeSouza would be dead within days.

I knew it but did nothing. There was a finality to the premonition. My revelation on the boat was of a possible outcome. This was of a definite, unchangeable future. Do not ask me how I knew. There are no words to explain.

And then the guerillas came. Boys, followed by the men from the forest tribes. They were all armed with tired rifles fired in wars fought long before the youngest had been born. Museum pieces. I have no idea why they shot DeSouza and not me. Perhaps they knew I would have to live with that guilt, a fate far worse than a bullet's quick and easy death. The Indian who shot DeSouza simply looked at me, then turned and went.

I had fled to the New World to escape the nausea and the blackouts and the violence they brought. And now I faced an equal but opposite curse. Aware before the event, I had effectively caused another man's death. Not through action, but inaction.

***

I offered Herzog and Darton an abridged and bowdlerized version of events. I omitted the incident in the engine room during the ocean crossing. And I made no reference to DeSouza's slaughter, implying our paths had simply diverged at the start of the insurrection. Whilst I was telling my tale, I glanced at Darton, opposite me. His face, glazed over like a lake in winter, showed a man otherwise occupied. There was an otherworldliness about his eyes, unfocused, staring in the general direction of the doctor's wife next to him. His lower lip hung loose, trembling, and he was breathing in shallow snatched breaths. His hands rested under the table. He began to shake, to judder.

I wanted to alert the doctor, to tell him Darton was heading towards some sort of fit. But Herzog was too busy with his own recollections of the revolution as told through the newspapers. He roared and slapped his thigh, wide eyes reaching up to the ceiling to illustrate a point, his arm making a frenzied arc through the heavens. I guessed he was trying to put the comments about bankruptcy behind him.

Meanwhile, Darton sat silently, eyes fixed, muscles clenched so tight they were spasming. His wife smiled child-like, a mask of polite interest, her mind no doubt busy with other tasks, like engineering our exit.

"...of course, what you could never have realized, what we only knew about through diplomatic sources..." Herzog continued, unaware I had long since stopped listening. He flourished his glass, splashing red wine. His wife's eyes glanced down at the offending spot as Darton rocked his head back, face screwed up, gums showing, and released a primal groan. Herzog's wife let out a scream of her own and leapt from her chair, cutting short her husband's theatrical tirade.

I jumped up, too, an unthinking reflex. Darton had managed to loosen his trousers, which now hung around his thighs. Herzog's wife stared down at herself, at the thin glistening greenish-white string of jism across her dress, leading back over his thigh, to Darton's cock. Her lips tried to form words, but no sounds came. Her head shook at the utter incomprehension of it. She glowered first at Darton, then at her husband, then lastly at me, as though blaming us all.

Darton panted, smiling, his face uncaring, as he pulled his trousers up.

"You... You..."

Gathering her dress, Herzog's wife rushed into the kitchen. It was unclear where she had directed the words. No doubt at Darton, but at Herzog, too, for inviting him? At me as well for doing...what? Perhaps, for doing nothing?

Herzog, in the manner of a man who is most animated when action is unnecessary, sat boss-eyed and open-mouthed throughout. There was not one flicker as he processed the near-impossible information: that Darton had just ejaculated over his wife in the middle of dinner. It was all far too horrible.

From the kitchen came the sound of crying. Short, snatched sobs. Herzog was torn between dealing with Darton and attending to his wife. With a glare, he marched into the kitchen.

Darton had the look of a man who had to work quickly. He leaned over the table towards me. "You know what you are doing here, don't you? You know what this is all about?"

"You're not mad."

He looked at me blankly.

"You're just pretending. It's not even a good act. You're just a pantomime crazy..."

"Who said I was mad? Nobody's said I'm mad. Except you." And then he gripped my wrist so hard it hurt. "Have you heard of the CIA?"

"What?"

"CIA. The Central Intelligence Agency."

I twisted myself free. "What have they got to do with anything..."

"But you've heard of them?" he insisted.

"Ancient history, twentieth, early twenty-first century..."

He cackled at that, his shoulders shaking, as if I had just said something exceptionally foolish. "They still exist. Like some ancient cult, like the pyramid builders, or whoever put those heads on Rapa Nui. The Pulse did not kill them. They have been gathering people changed by the Pulse, following their children and their children's children. You. Me. Herzog's job was to see what the Pulse did to us. You are different, yes? You know you are, yes? It was Herzog's job to see how your abilities developed. But you left him. You were the prize asset, and you left him. Then the CIA cut him off. If he doesn't get us back, he's as good as dead. He has debts..."

He was cut off by Herzog bursting from the kitchen, a poker in his hand. "Get out," he bawled.

For a second, a ridiculous tableau presented itself. Herzog, arm raised, ready to bring the fire iron down on Darton. Darton, one arm held high for protection, his other hand trying to button his fly.

"Get out, or, by Christ, I don't know what I'll do!"

Darton reeled backwards towards the door. "You want money. Well, you have my seed instead," he spat.

"Get out!" Herzog let fly with the poker, missing Darton by an inch.

Darton fell, slithering backwards. "I'm a sick man, doctor. You've told me that yourself."

"Don't let your mind excuse your body, you filth. Get out."

And with that, Darton picked himself up off the floor and fled into the snowy night.

Herzog's poker remained ready to strike long after the door had slammed shut. Wearily, his arm drooped.

"I should go."

"No. Stay a while," he insisted. "Although I fear my wife will not be joining us for the remainder of the evening. Will you take another Becherovka?"

Pouring two measures, he asked, "So, how are you? How are you really, Jon?"

So, was this it? A medical check-up, a post-treatment review of my progress. Was this his way of closing the book on what had just happened? Psychiatrists need coping mechanisms too.

"No repetition of your previous symptoms? No blackouts? No episodes of violence?"

The medical profession's ability to ask the most personal and sensitive of questions as though ordering a cut of meat has never ceased to amaze. Even my closest friends would—could—only allude to such a question by way of euphemisms and sideways looks.

I paused, silently coming to an arbitrary decision, as if mentally tossing a coin.

"I killed a man. In South America."

"A man has to defend himself..."

I silenced the doctor. "I killed DeSouza. Not through blackouts. I was aware of everything that happened. All too aware. Forget what I told you about how it ended. It didn't happen like I said at all."

And the story just spilled out of me, from the incident in the engine room onwards. I had no idea why I wanted to open up to Herzog, why now, after what Darton had told me. Perhaps because I didn't believe a word of it. Sharing was a show of faith in Herzog.

After I had finished, Herzog was quiet for a long time. He stared into the dull butter-colored Becherovka, swilling and swirling it back and forth. "You feel guilt for his death, but you saved his life. Perhaps twice."

"I know. I've thought about that, but I do not think the two cancel themselves out. You can't set one against the other."

Herzog held up his glass, considering the color of the fire through the spirit. "Your gift, for that is what it is, is incredible. I had no idea your condition could develop in such a direction. There is something I would like to show you. Something that, given your story, you may find interesting. Come."

He rose and made his way up the curving staircase to the upper floor. My head felt heavy with drink. Herzog, eager, trotted before me. By the time I had reached the top step, I could only catch a glimpse of him going into a room off the upper landing, nothing more than a flurry of jacket tails and the flick of a trailing shoe.

The room was Herzog's private study, lit by candlelight and decorated in dark colors. It gave the room a morbid air, the walls seeming to shimmer slightly. He held out a dossier of papers to me, a single sheet of buff card folded in two and held shut with a string running from the middle of one cover, over the longest edge, to the middle of the opposing side where it was looped over and over again around a small button. The papers inside made the whole package about the thickness of two fingers.

"Open it," Herzog said.

"Before I open it, I want to know one thing."

Herzog looked quizzical.

"How did you know that I was here?"

"I knew you went to South America and that you would have had to leave. I thought you may return here, but really didn't think you would. I had the passenger manifests of ships arriving in the harbor sent to me. There aren't that many. It was a simple matter to find your lodgings after that."

"But why?"

"Because what Darton said was true," he blurted, and for a moment I thought he was referring to Darton's bizarre references to the Central Intelligence Agency. "I am bankrupt. Totally wiped out. Bad investments. Many in South America. So, really, I suffered the same maelstrom you did. Only here, in the comfort of my own home. A home I can barely afford. Plus, the cost of my collection."

"Your collection?"

Herzog glanced down at the dossier by way of explanation before continuing. "From what little we heard, you came away with a fortune. A silver mine, we were told."

"Ice."

"Silver, we heard."

"Darton was right. It all melted. I came away with nothing more than what was in my pockets."

He brightened with hope. "But you still have money here? Your family?"

"You thought you could touch me for money?"

The irony of such a reversal, that once I came to him in daylight for his help, whereas now I had been summoned at night to help him, was not lost on me. I'd come hoping it would be him lending me money, not me him. I couldn't help but laugh in his face.

He hung his head. "My last hopes were you and Darton. Darton is rich. Rich and disgusting."

"And I'm not rich. I came back in steerage. I ate fish soup and potatoes and bread that was green by the time we landed."

He smiled placatingly. "Let us talk of it no longer. 'Never a borrower nor a lender be', is that not how it goes? My troubles are my troubles. Yours are yours." He gently slapped my shoulder, a brotherly gesture. As he did so, he indicated the buff folder once more, urging me to open it.

I unwound the string from the button and gently opened the folder. Revealed was a stack of handwritten notes, more than a hundred in number. I turned them over, one by one. The majority were no more than a single side. Some covered two sides. One ran to ten pages of tight, looped characters. Each, different to its predecessor. Each written on paper of a different quality and color. Each written by a different hand, most signed, several not.

Some looked fresh, some were stained and faded with age. Phrases thrust themselves before me:

"*I cannot go on.*"

"*I am sorry, truly sorry.*"

"*Forgive me.*"

There was pain in the words. Pain, fear, and anguish.

"What do you feel when you read them?"

"Nothing," I replied. "Nothing at all."

"Not a thing?" He seemed bemused.

"I feel blackness, darkness, emptiness. I feel like I did before DeSouza died. But the feeling is weaker, like a faded bruise."

"Like a faded bruise," Herzog repeated, washing the words around in his mouth like a fine wine. "Suicide notes. They are all the notes of victims of suicide. People driven to take their own lives."

"So many."

"I believe it to be one of the largest private collections in the country. Maybe the largest. There has come on to the market a particularly rare piece." Herzog's voice had become breathless with excitement. "As much a confession as a suicide note. Of a particularly high-ranking figure from a forgotten era. Cartier, I need money to buy it. I must have it."

I stared wide-eyed at him.

"It is not the nature of the confession which interests me. The note would have caused scandal had it emerged a hundred years ago, but now it is only of historical significance. I want it purely to add to a private collection. You must see that."

I felt giddy with sickness. Herzog's face was ruddy, shiny with sweat. His shoulders rose and fell with each breath. As I stared at him, he began to go in and out of focus. The room, already dark, dimmed further. He started to slip away. He jabbered in the distance, arms waving, but almost silent now, his voice engulfed by the sound of roaring in my ears.

I knew what this was. I knew what this meant. I knew the kind of madness that was returning to me. I gripped the side of the table on which Doctor Herzog's collection lay. I felt my knuckles turning white, felt the pain a long way away.

Herzog's voice echoed. "I need money, Cartier. Two million. Two and a half at the outside. Can you get it for me? Borrow it if needs be. My creditors are... I cannot ask them again." His voice was clearer now. The rush had passed. There would be no blackout, for the moment at least.

The doctor seemed oblivious of how near to collapse he had pushed me, of the effect his hysteria had on me, even though we had discussed such episodes ad nauseum whilst I was under his care. Nearly crimson himself, he paced up and down and kept on and on about the price he would have to pay for this, the nadir, the zenith of his perverted collection. Then he stopped and, as possessed as Darton had been in his ravings about the CIA, declared. "You are a gambling man, Cartier." The sheer momentum of his mood meant he couldn't wait for a reply. "Place a wager upon my collection."

"I don't understand."

"One of the notes in my collection is not what it purports to be. One of the suicide notes is not a suicide note. Its author is alive and well. And talking to you."

"You have written a suicide note?"

"Ah, no." He wagged a warning finger. "A subtle distinction. It is not a suicide note. It merely appears to be a suicide note. A satirical exercise, or maybe a dabbling attempt at forgery. Now, I'm not even sure myself why I wrote it. You made it sound like something I'm holding in reserve for a rainy day."

"Not even as a bankrupt?"

The words appeared to sting him, and I feared being thrown out as Darton had been. The moment soon passed. "The wager is this. Using your skill at predicting an individual's future from their handwriting, look at my collection, and tell me which was penned by the person still living. Still living and not about to die."

I began to laugh again.

Herzog persisted. "The immediate future of all those who wrote the notes, the real notes, was death. In all cases, they took their own lives within moments. Some poisoned themselves, others hanged themselves. Some drowned. Slit wrists, slashed necks. Pistol to the temple. If you can tell the future from their hand, then that future is still in their notes."

"Old futures. What anybody else would call the past."

"But you said yourself that you could feel it," he persisted.

I took a moment to consider. He was correct. I had the bitter aftertaste of the authors' suicidal tendencies, of their now-ancient future deaths, in my mouth.

"Why?"

"You want a reason? Let us say for the sake of scientific experiment. Let us say that I do not believe your claim. Or, at the very least, I am suspicious. I want to verify it. This is an experiment to test whether you can identify a rogue element from within a sea of strong stimuli."

Herzog had immense pride in his Machiavellian machinations. "But was DeSouza's experiment with the cards not good enough for your purposes?"

"That was DeSouza's experiment. This is mine. And, anyway, DeSouza is no longer with us to report the results firsthand. If I win, you give me, let us say, five million. Easily enough to purchase the letter of which I speak, as well as covering a number of debts."

"I do not have five million," I said plainly.

"You can get hold of it. Your family."

I didn't have the energy to argue his point.

"But, if you win, you take the house."

I looked in amazement at him. "Your house?"

He laughed, a crone-like cackle. "I feel confident."

I considered the proposition. Putting aside where I was to get five million from, what if I won? What would I do with Herzog's house? It was far too large for me to live here. Would I allow the doctor to continue to reside here, maintain his practice and public face? But, if he were bankrupt, what rent could he pay me? Would I have the steel to throw Herzog and his wife out into the street, into the snow? Then there was the question of whether the house was Herzog's to wager away, or whether it was already the bank's...

"Are you playing then?" Herzog demanded, by now quite breathless.

"Yes."

"Then I will bring two more Becherovkas and you will leaf through the papers again. And then you will give me your answer at your leisure."

I sat and, as before, considered each note in turn. It was a collection that chilled me to the bone. I realized the stains I had seen on one letter to a child were salty tears. Ink blobs were spatterings of blood. In a very real sense, I imagined pens being replaced in inkwells, then glasses of bitter liquid being drained, eyes looking up at a noose, or a clumsy grip taken on a pistol in the mouth. Some tried to explain, their logic as variable in their clarity as my premonitions. Others said nothing about their reasons. If I learnt one thing in South America, it was to never question why. I was no longer impressed or amazed by what the human animal is capable of.

I had gone through each and every note. Herzog held out yet another tumbler of Becherovka. My head was already swimming with drink. And each one of the suicide notes told me of nothing other than death. Some as raw as lemon in a wound, some just faded scars.

"Well?" Herzog demanded.

"I...I do not know."

Herzog began to laugh again, a coarse, grating snigger. It felt like fingers on a child's balloon, nails running down a chalkboard.

I leafed through the suicide notes again. There was nothing. Just void. Vacuum. An abyss where there should have been the hum of life. A stark indigo chasm. Too distant to be painful, but clear, nonetheless. On each and every one.

"Which one? Which one?" Herzog cried triumphantly.

I stared back in bewildered confusion. Every letter spelt death.

The doctor's voice grew distant, washed over by another sound, that of my lungs straining for air. And then I was falling. Falling into a dark kaleidoscopic tunnel, a well, back first, face uppermost. Herzog, the letters, the room were shrinking. Blackness was closing in on me.

"I do not know. I do not know." Distantly, I recognized my own voice.

Herzog was leaping around the room with one particular note in his hand, written on yellowing paper, aged artificially. "You see? You see?"

I watched him passively. A weight had been thrust upon my chest. He was grabbing anything—scribbled note, diary entry, medical record—upon which his handwriting was visible. His distant voice had risen a further octave.

"You see? It is my handwriting. Mine. My own. Were you looking for the handwriting on the invitation? Ha! That was written by my wife."

My head buzzed. Flies crawled over my skull, pulling at my hair and scalp with their scaly feet. My skin felt like it was moving, like the flies were pulling it down so that it would cover my eyes and my nose and my mouth, so I wouldn't be able to see or breathe or cry out.

"You want more proof?" He leant over me, spitting in my face in his ecstasy. I could feel it on my cheeks. "You want more proof? I'll sign it."

And there before me he chose a fountain pen, and with a swirling, confident hand signed it. *Cornelius Marcus Herzog.*

***

Herzog's wife found me two hours later, unconscious in the freezing room, the snow billowing in. She had been woken by the cold draft. She had roused me, then closed the windows that opened out onto the street. It was then she saw the snow-covered body of Doctor Herzog, comically skewered on the iron railings below, his back impossibly arched.

I had little memory of the final events of the night. Or rather, I had several memories, splintered, disjointed, and contradictory. I had the sense to say her husband had struck me cold, and that was the last I remembered. It was an element of the story I stuck to when Bertrand arrived, an eyebrow raised when he saw it was me. For all I knew, it may have been the truth.

Given my history, I could hardly complain at his attempt to pin Herzog's death on me. But there was too much circumstantial evidence—the doctor's financial position, the fact Darton and I were not the first people he had wined and dined in the hope of raising ready cash, and, not least, the note—for them to conclude anything other than suicide. They even called Darton in. He sneered at them and told them a variety of fictions of varying degrees of ludicrousness before they threw him out.

After a suitable period, I made plans to leave the city with only one mystery remaining for Bertrand to solve: the hundred and seventy-eight other suicide notes found fluttering in the snow.

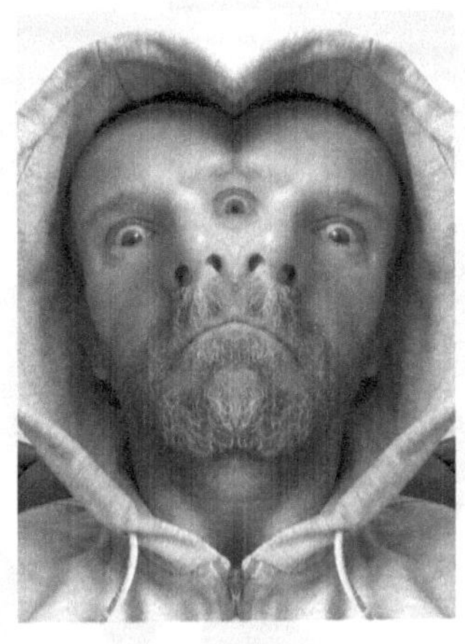

Robert Bagnall was born in Bedford, England, in 1970 and stood for parliament for the Green Party in 2024. He has written for the BBC, national newspapers, and government ministers. Five of his stories have been selected for the annual *Best of British Science Fiction* anthologies. He is the author of sci-fi thriller *2084 - The Meschera Bandwidth* and two anthologies, each of which collects 24 of his ninety-odd published stories.

meschera.blogspot.com

# CONTENT WARNINGS

*Standard warnings for horror tropes (violence, death, murder) apply to all Graveside Press books.*

references to suicide
sexual harassment and lewd conduct

*Thank you for supporting Graveside Press and our authors.*
*One of the biggest ways you can help is to leave a star rating*
*or a review wherever you purchased your copy!*

# STAY SPOOKY.

Want merch, membership benefits, and discounts on
Graveside books?
gsp-shop.fourthwall.com

Wanna come hang out with the ghouls?
gravesidepress.carrd.co